WHO AM I?

Library and Archives Canada Cataloguing in Publication

Bharucha, Jasmine, 1969-, author
        Who am I? / Jasmine Bharucha ; illustrator, Maggie

J.H. Wang.

ISBN 978-1-77141-067-0 (pbk.)

        1. Identity (Psychology)--Juvenile literature. I. Wang,

Maggie J. H., 1976-, illustrator II. Title.

BF697.B43 2014   j155.2   C2014-904807-6

WHO AM I?

An Interactive Guide to **Self-Discovery** for Kids and Parents

Jasmine Bharucha

First Published in Canada 2014 by Influence Publishing

Illustrator/Graphic Designer: Maggie J. H. Wang
Typeset: Greg Salisbury
Author Photographer: Sandra Steier

DISCLAIMER: This book is a guide intended to offer information on how to connect with oneself and others. It is not intended in any way to replace other professional health care or mental health advice, but to support it. Readers of this publication agree that neither the author nor her publisher will be held responsible or liable for damages that may be alleged or resulting directly or indirectly from the reading of this publication.

For my children—Éva and Noble.

For the children of the world.

For the inner child.

Testimonials

"*Who Am I?* by Jasmine Bharucha is a wonderful book that introduces the concept of how we are all connected to the world. This book teaches children that they are not alone and are an unlimited part of the universe where they live and grow. It is an excellent resource to support the concept of mindfulness in our busy classrooms."
Sue Stevenson, Principal, Carnarvon Elementary School

"This book offers parents simple explanations for those difficult questions often posed by children."
Karrie Beauchamp, ECE Coordinator, Crofton House School

"This is a beautiful book with simple yet timeless truths, perfect for teaching children how to tap into their amazing potential."
Sherry Strong, Food Philosopher, Author of *Return to Food*

Introduction

1. Before you start to read this book, sit in a quiet spot and notice your breathing.

2. Read each page very slowly and do not allow yourself to be distracted.

3. After you finish reading, write down any feelings and thoughts in a journal.

4. It is very easy for us to forget who we are. Reading this book daily will help you remember who you are.

5. Reading this book alone allows you your own experience.

6. Reading this book with someone else will be a shared experience and different every time.

Jasmine Bharucha

The  is a

living organism

to which nothing can be added

exccept the rays of the SUN

Earth only

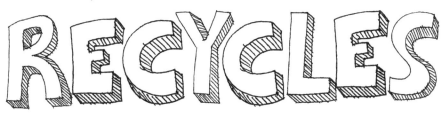

RECYCLES

what already exists.

Our planet Earth is made up of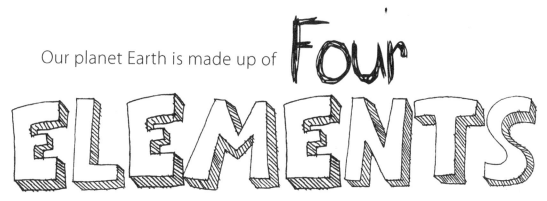

Fire, Water, Air, and Earth.

Today, you are going to learn that the Earth has a fifth element

" S p a c e "

You and everything around you is made up of these five elements.

Together, these elements support Life.

What is the fifth element called

SPACE ?

Space is NOT nothing.

Space is energy that cannot be seen by the human eye.

It is the glue that connects everything together.

It cannot be weighed or measured.

We know there is gravity. We cannot see gravity, but we feel it,

as it keeps us bound to the planet.

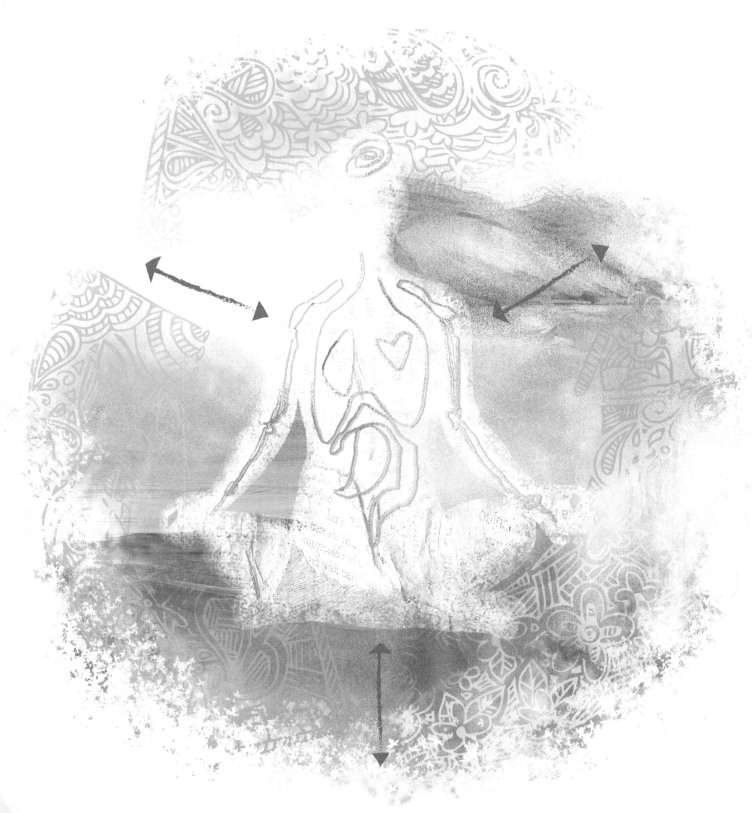

The entire body,

Skin, Organs, Nails, Hair RECYCLES back to the planet.

So, there is a little bit of

YOU in

EVERYTHING and a little bit of

EVERYTHING

in YOU

When you show your love and take care of the planet, you are loving and taking care of yourself. And everything on the

PLANET

loves and cares for you.

Nothing is separated.
We are all connected.
We are all 1

Our planet exists among other Planets, Stars, and Solar Systems as part of the whole …

Without the Sun warming us with its rays, we would not exist.

The entire Universe exists and depends on everything **within** it.

Hence, we are one with the Universe ... we are

What does it mean to be LIMITLESS and INFINITE?

It means to have

No Beginning and No End.

to be Everything and Nothing.

To be All Powerful and Immeasurable.

WHO AM I?

I am an **Infinite**, **Limitless being** in a **Limited body**.

I AM NOT SEPARATE.
I AM NEVER ALONE.
I AM CONNECTED.

I AM SAFE.

Q & A for Me and My Family

1. **What is the difference between my limited and unlimited selves?**

   My limited self is my body and it includes my mind, which creates my thoughts. My limited self is always evaluating the present through the past and the future. My limited self feels fear.

   My unlimited self only lives in the present moment. It does not live in the past or the future. My unlimited self does not think and judge. It accepts what is and treats every situation as an opportunity to grow and learn.

1. **What happens to us when we die?**

   Everything around you has energy. The body is the physical shell that holds the energy. The body you are in has been chosen for this life.
   When you die your energy still lives; it goes back into the energy of the Universe. Your physical body returns back into the planet.

2. **What do I do when I feel alone?**

   Remember that you are never alone. You are connected with nature and your body all the time. The reason you feel alone is because you choose what you want to connect with and what you do not want to connect with, instead of accepting what is present right now.

Nothing happens to you, it happens for you. When one connection is lost, another one is always available, if you are open to receiving it. No one can hold you and love you more than you can love yourself.
Put your arms around yourself and give yourself a hug.
Know that you are perfect exactly the way you are and that the world would be incomplete without you.

4. **What happens when somebody doesn't want to connect with me?**
You cannot control who chooses to connect with you. Connecting and separating is a natural part of life. Remember never to take it personally. If you do, you will get caught up in the feeling of separation and become a victim of it.

When we feel separate, it is a great opportunity to connect inside ourselves and see where we reject ourselves.

What do I not like about myself?

Can I accept that part of myself?

Do I see that even the part of me I reject makes me who I am?

Put your arms around yourself, give that part of you a hug and thank that part of you.

Having done this, go back out into the world. Look around, there is always another connection ready to start, as soon as you are ready.

Your DAILY Journal

1.
What did I like about today?

2.
What did I not like about today?

1a. How did it make me feel?

2a. How did it make me feel?

_____

_____

_____

_____

_____

_____

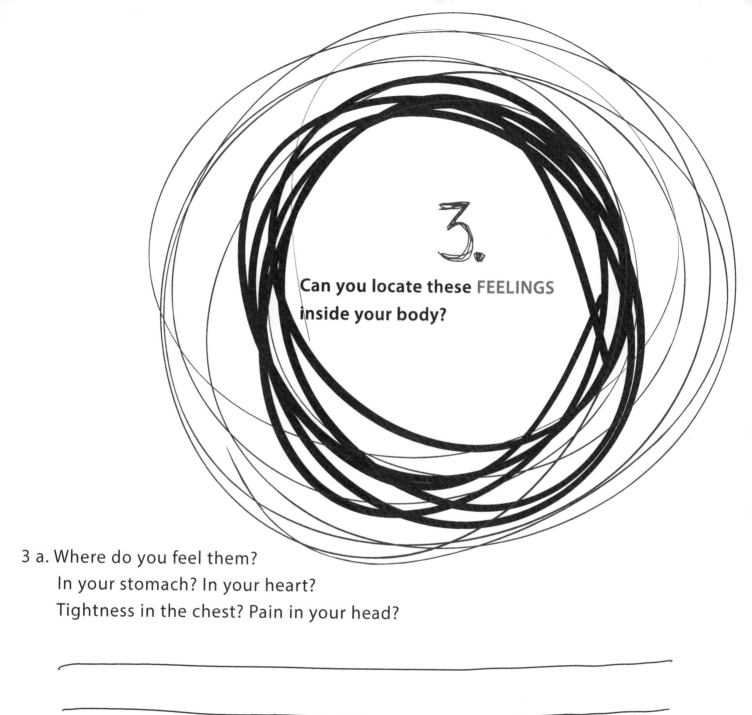

3.

Can you locate these FEELINGS inside your body?

3 a. Where do you feel them?
In your stomach? In your heart?
Tightness in the chest? Pain in your head?

Would You Like to CONNECT with Your Unlimited Self ?

Step 1:

Sit down in a quiet spot with your hands resting on your knees.

Step 2:

Hold your palms up, in the shape of a cup.

Your cups are empty and ready to be filled with peace and calm.

Step 3:

Close your eyes and notice any pain or discomfort in your body.

Move your attention from your toes, to your knees, to your hips, to

your stomach, to your throat, and all the way to the top of your head.

Step 4:

Shift your attention to the tip of your nose. Observe your breath as it enters your nose and observe the breath as it leaves you. Notice that it takes no effort to breathe. You can now release any feelings of pain or discomfort through your breath.

Step 5:

If you feel the urge to cry, go ahead and release your tears. Releasing tears also helps you release any anger or sadness that is hidden in your body. Stay with your breath as long as you choose.

Step 6:

Sitting in this place is like sitting in your inner garden. When the outside world becomes difficult, visit your inner garden. This is where you can let go of your thoughts and connect with your unlimited self. Visiting the garden daily means your garden will grow and so will your feelings of peace.

GLOSSARY

Bound: To be held to something.

Earth: The planet we live on.

Elements: The 5 building blocks of life—Fire, Water, Air, Earth, and Space.

Energy: A vibration that cannot be created or destroyed.

Exist: To have life.

Gravity: A force that keeps a body bound to the planet.

Immeasurable: What cannot be measured.

Infinite: Impossible to measure.

Limitless: Being without end or boundary.

Organism: A living thing.

Recycle: To use again.

Universe: Everything that exists in and around us.

Within: Everything inside.

Jasmine Bharucha is an author, mother of two and an internationally renowned singer/songwriter who was the first Indian performer to appear on MTV Asia in 1990. She has been featured in Rolling Stone Magazine, Time Magazine and other international media, and has been nominated as the Best Female Pop Artist at the Channel V Music Awards in Asia.

As a child growing up in Mumbai, India, Bharucha would often ask questions about why some children lived in such dire poverty and she didn't—she was always trying to make sense of the puzzle of life.

Her journey of self-reflection fuelled her studies in holistic medicine and life coaching. Her exploration led her to ask the basic question: "Who Am I?" This question then translated into the title of her first children's book, *Who Am I?*, that presents simple concepts for children, and adults too, to better understand themselves and their connection to the world around them. Believing that it's never too early or too late to start the self-inquiry process, Bharucha speaks about and shares this message today with young and old alike.

She currently lives in Vancouver, Canada, with her husband and two children, where she works as an award-winning realtor and continues to sing and perform.

If you want to get on the path to be a published author by
Influence Publishing please go to
www.InfluencePublishing.com

Inspiring books that influence change

More information on our other titles and how to submit your own proposal
can be found at
www.InfluencePublishing.com

CPSIA information can be obtained at www.ICGtesting.com
Printed in the USA
LVOW02s2126221014

410055LV00001B/4/P